MARIE-HÉLÈNE LEBEAULT
AUTHOR OF THE EVERS SERIES

A SUMMER
OF
DESTINY

DEFENDERS OF THE REALM - NOVELLA FOUR

About the Author

Marie-Helene Lebeault lives in Quebec, Canada and is the mother of two young adults. A retired teacher, she now spends her days writing, translating academic manuals, and lending her voice to corporate training videos. She enjoys reading, hiking, and going to the beach. She is also an avid rollercoaster fiend and is on a mission to visit all the Six Flags amusement parks with her daughter. Every year, she travels for three weeks on a solo adventure to a new part of the world.

Follow on Social Media, she'd love to hear from you!

Website Email Newsletter

facebook.com/mhlebeaultauthor

x.com/mhlebeault

instagram.com/mhlebeault

amazon.com/author/mhlebeault

bookbub.com/authors/marie-helene-lebeault

goodreads.com/mhlebeault

linkedin.com/in/mhlebeault

tiktok.com/@mhlebeaultauthor

youtube.com/@mhlebeault

Also by the Author

The Chronicles of the Starborne Cadets

Stars Beyond Realms

Shadows of Orion

Echoes of the Void

The Nebula's Heart

The Starborne Paradox

Defenders of the Realm

A Journey to Power

The Quest for the Emerald Rattleback

A Summer of Discovery

The Quest for the Sacred Tree

A Summer of Opposites

The Quest for the Phantom Feather

A Summer of Courage

The Quest for the Kraken's Ink

A Summer of Destiny

The Quest for the Cursed Mirrors

The Evers Series

The Ancestors' Key

The Academy

The Time Walker

The World Jumper

Blood Magick Trilogy

The Blood Mage

Blood Magick

Blood Legacy

Standalones

Clarity Castle

What Happens Next?

Ghost Stories

Holiday Shifters

Echoes of Tomorrow

Utopia

Picture Books

Fairy Grandmother: Millie Goes to Antarctica

Fairy Grandmother: Millie Goes to the North Pole

Fairy Grandmother: Millie Goes to China

Fairy Grandmother: Millie Goes to Africa

(Also available in French, Spanish, German, and Italian)

CHAPTER

ONE

Raven straightened from where they were sweeping out a cabin. Their back was aching from the hunched position they had been in—the broom was just a little too short for them. Not that they minded so much. This was nothing compared to the constant pain they had once been in.

They stepped outside of the cabin, lifting their veiled face to the sky. It was a cool day, and the thin fabric was so light that it was as though they weren't wearing anything at all. The biggest problem was the fact that the veil also covered their eyes. Luckily, one of their witch friends, Kaia, was clever with her spells and enchanted the fabric so Raven could see through it.

After a hectic semester, Raven was relieved to be at the Silent Marshes with Penelope and their parents.

It was a beautiful space. Even at the start of the year, deep in midwinter, the marshes were a vibrant green. Birds and other creatures called to each other, and there was a sweetness to the air that Raven eagerly drank in.

"Are you done with that cabin?" their mother asked.

Raven turned, surprised they hadn't heard their mother approaching. She wore a sleeveless tunic and shorts. Even though their mother always preferred cool weather over hot, she seemed amused by Raven's attire. Raven had to admit it had been a hot, dry winter so far. There was snow in other regions, but here it was still so warm.

"I'm just taking a break to stretch my back," Raven told their mother.

The four of them—Mom, Dad, Penelope, and Raven—had been asked to prepare the cabins for when the first-year witches would arrive. It was a task they all found to be meaningful. And while they were all together, Raven had the opportunity to collect the shed skin of the giant, magnificent Emerald Rattleback.

All witches needed the skin for their spell books. And while Raven was a gorgon, not a witch, their magic was closer to that of a witch than dragon.

So Raven was catching up on the lessons they had missed. Since they had only gotten their powers two years ago, they had to come to the Silent Marshes to get the emerald Rattleback skin. Then, they would head to the Golden Forest to collect wood from the Phoenix Ginkgo to make paper for their book and finally...

They shook their head. There was no use in worrying about the Thunder Mountains. Not yet.

"Raven?" Mom's face fell into that familiar look of worry. "Do you need a rest?"

Raven shook their head again. "I'm fine. I just got distracted, thinking about everything that needs to be done around here."

Mom hurried forward and took the broom from their hand. "Why don't you have a little rest while I finish here?"

The worry shone from Mom's face, and Raven didn't have the heart to argue. They handed the broom and then headed toward the well in the middle of the camp. They rigged it with a pump, which made drawing water easier, and Raven filled buckets.

The cleaning crew needed to heat the water, as there had been evidence of mice in a few of the cabins. Everything needed to be scrubbed down well to ensure it was good and clean for the students.

As they were drawing the water, though, they were interrupted.

"You shouldn't be doing that," their father said, hurrying over. He hefted a full bucket in each hand as he jerked his chin toward the cabin the four had been sleeping in. "Why don't you go rest, Raven?"

Raven propped their hands on their hips. "First, Mom won't let me sweep, and now you're trying to stop me from drawing water? I told you, I'm not sick anymore. I don't need—"

"We don't want you to get sick again," Dad interrupted.

Raven groaned. "Dad—"

They leaned in to continue their argument, but as they did so, the pump handle came up, seemingly by itself. It caught the edge of their face veil and yanked it upward.

Raven threw both hands over their face, keeping the cloth in place as they stumbled backward. Their heart slammed into their ribs as an awful taste crept up their throat. At that moment, the only thing they wanted to do was get out of there.

"Er, sorry," they mumbled as they continued to back away.

Dad came forward, looking concerned, but Raven held out a hand to him.

"I'm fine. You're right. I'm tired. I will go... go rest," Raven said, fighting to keep their voice even and calm. They failed terribly, and tears pricked against their eyes. Dad couldn't see their tears, but he could hear them in their voice.

"Raven," Dad said, putting down the buckets.

"I'm fine," Raven said, then turned on their heel and swiftly marched away.

That was too close. Despite their precautions, if their veil came off, anyone would see their face.

They followed a path into the marshes, winding their way into the green paradise until they found the low bench that was magically maintained. There, they sat and pressed their hands to the warm wood as they lifted their face to the sky.

Before they had figured out what they had become, they had turned several deer and other woodland creatures into stone. Just by the creatures looking into their face. If that had happened with their parents...

A sick feeling twisted in their stomach as they attempted to regulate themselves.

Last semester, after being held prisoner by the mermaid queen Lyra for months, Raven learned that this wasn't a curse. No, gorgons had originally been the protectors of the sea, according to the ancient, massive kraken, Tidebreaker.

That didn't mean they had entirely accepted this reality. Most times, they could live almost normally. But somehow, being around their parents made it even more stark. Life would never be the same as it once was, and Raven wasn't sure if they would ever be comfortable with this.

They couldn't show their face again, but they felt different, too. Raven had never been entirely comfortable in their body. But they always thought it was the way everyone felt a little uncomfortable with their perceived flaws.

Now, though, they felt different. It wasn't anything they could fully put their finger on. Perhaps their skin was more sensitive. Or maybe their hair had been transformed to feathery gills, each with their own sense of what was occurring around them.

On land, these gills were encased in a hard, scaly shell that resembled snakes and sometimes even writhed like legless creatures. Maybe it was because of this that Raven always felt like they were overly dry, and no amount of drinking water helped to ease that feeling.

And everything was so loud. Even here in the 'Silent' Marshes. The buzzing was relentless, and Odele thought it was Raven's heightened connection to her surroundings due to being a gorgon of the sea.

It made sense in that respect. They couldn't speak the same way under the water, so having increased mind-to-mind communication skills was useful. It helped while the students attempted to negotiate peace between the krakens and mermaids.

Feeling calmer now, Raven leaned back against the bench.

In the end, they knew that this wasn't a punishment. While it certainly felt like one at first, that was partly due to not understanding the actual situation. The Silver Springs connected them to the earth's magic, and they no longer felt they were being punished for seeking a new type of magic.

But it still felt like a curse. In their stories, Raven understood why the ancient gorgons lived in isolated caves. It was a terrible feeling that any minor accident would turn their friends or loved ones into statues.

Of course, that wasn't information they could share with anyone, not with their parents, the Headmasters at the Institute, or even Penelope.

The thing about these feelings was that they weren't something that could be fixed. And no amount of reassurance would make it go away. If Raven did share how unhappy they were, it would only end up with those around them, trying to make them feel better.

Raven didn't want to feel better—they weren't sure it was possible. They just wanted to accept these feelings and learn how to continue despite them.

Raven heard footsteps approaching and checked to ensure their face veil was in place.

Soon after, Penelope came into view. As usual, she smiled at them and the tension eased from Raven's body at just seeing her.

"Jack said that you were upset," Penelope said as she slid onto the bench beside Raven.

She wore the plain blue uniform of the Institute that dragons were given. The uniform could be used for shifting forms without being damaged, and it would repair itself if torn. The students didn't have to wear them if they didn't want to, but Penelope had made a habit of wearing hers.

She planned to apply for the military once she graduated next year and said she needed to get used to wearing a uniform.

Raven knew it would be hard on both of them, but Penelope had planned this path before they met. Raven figured they'd have other career opportunities; they could work around their mate's military service.

"I did get upset," they said with a shrug. "Mom and Dad both are still treating me like their frail child. It's exhausting."

Penelope hummed. "Yeah, they seem to hover. Given how sick you always used to be, I guess it's understandable. It's a learning curve."

"Yeah."

Penelope's fire-red hair was so thick and beautiful that Raven loved to brush their fingers through it. Today, it was braided tightly and wound into a bun at the back of her head. It made her look more severe than she actually was.

In some ways, it made her look older, too. Sometimes it was difficult for Raven to remember that they were almost a year older than Penelope. Pen was just so confident in herself. It was like she always knew what to do.

Raven wished they could be more like that. But truthfully, they were still getting used to having options other than sitting at a window doing needlework.

Having the options was wonderful, but it was also overwhelming. Raven wasn't sure how something could be a positive and a negative all at once, and yet it was.

Penelope stood again and held a hand out to them. "Let's go explore a bit. Get your mind off things. What do you think?"

Raven smiled and took Penelope's hand. "That sounds amazing."

CHAPTER

TWO

Penelope led the way through the swamp, mindful to keep on the path so they could find their way back. She enjoyed the quiet of the surrounding space. It was a welcome change from the noise of the Institute.

It was cooler within the trees than it had been outside them, too. Penelope wished they had brought along a picnic, so she and Raven could spend more time here by themselves.

"What's that sound?" Raven asked suddenly. They reached out and grabbed Penelope's wrist, stopping her.

Penelope cocked her head, listening intently. The marshes had deep magic in them that made them absolutely silent to any person other than witches—and gorgons, apparently. "I don't hear a thing."

But even as she spoke, a soft buzzing noise entered her hearing. She turned just in time to see a swarm of brownies burst from the surrounding foliage. Their wings fluttered as they rose their tiny spears and charged toward the two teens.

Penelope immediately hummed, a low and deep sound just as Professor Farrow had taught her in her first year.

The brownies swarmed around the two and waved their spears, but didn't attack.

One of them flew into Penelope's face and angrily chattered at her.

"What are you talking about?" Raven asked.

The brownie retreated a couple of inches and turned to Raven, chattering again.

Raven tilted their head and raised their hands. "I don't know. It appears I can understand you, and you can understand me."

Penelope looked between the two with wide eyes. Whenever she thought she had a handle on Raven's powers, something new would appear like this. A smile formed on her lips, but she schooled her expression—the brownies seemed furious, and she didn't want to cause further trouble.

"What's going on?" she asked instead.

Raven turned slightly as the brownie continued to chatter on and on like an angry chipmunk. "Apparently, you were part of a big kerfuffle here a few years ago. You and a bunch of others camped outside their nest, and then others came and there was a bunch of... er, fighting, I guess. It's a little unclear."

Penelope stared at the brownies. No way. "You mean these are the same brownies disturbed when Finnegan and Odentia attempted to kidnap Adina?"

The brownie brandished its spear and chattered.

"Those words sound familiar," Raven said. "And they're upset that you never came back to fix up what you broke."

Penelope could have laughed; only the situation was certainly not that funny. She rubbed the back of her neck. Penelope couldn't recall breaking any brownie nests, but she supposed that wasn't the issue. She'd had so much on her mind at the time that she hadn't exactly paid much attention to anything other than keeping herself and her friends alive.

"I know it's been a long time, but if they have anything that they'd like me to help them build now, I can do that," she finally offered. The last thing she wanted was to be attacked whenever she came into the marshes.

Besides that, she damaged their property in the past. The least she could do now was try to make amends. It didn't matter if it was on purpose or not, or if she had been a child.

Raven relayed her words to the brownies, who huddled together in a chattering, buzzing swarm several feet away. A few of them waved their spears over their heads but most stowed them away.

One of them came back over and circled Penelope. It grabbed the end of her fiery-red braid and pulled it over her shoulder as though trying to lead her by it. She followed while Raven stuck tightly next to her side.

She smiled amusedly at her mate but didn't know if Raven saw it.

And all at once, her gut squeezed. Raven hadn't been a gorgon until Penelope went into her third year. But the ceremony to reveal fated mates—a perfect or bonded match—was at the end of the second year.

Penelope had gone through the ceremony to have no mate revealed. And even now, when she was entirely dedicated to Raven and everything they had been through together. She sometimes wondered if the stars had bonded them because neither had anyone else.

Was it a perfect match, or just the match that happened to be together?

She schooled her expression and pushed the thought away. She had been doing her best not to let Raven see her doubts. Raven was going through so much already. The last thing they needed was to know that their bonded mate wasn't sure that they were actually meant to be together.

No. Even if they were matched 'just because,' it didn't mean their connection was any less real. Anything else was inconsequential.

Soon, the two of them had gotten to the brownie nest. The brownies buzzed around, gesturing to various sticks and stones lying about. Penelope had difficulty keeping track of individual brownies, and Raven kept saying something and then stopping.

Finally, Penelope lifted both of her hands. The brownies shied back from her, and a few pointed their spears.

"Can you tell them I don't understand what they want me to do?" she asked Raven.

Raven repeated her words, and a cacophony of chattering responded.

"No, no," Raven said, raising their voice to be heard over the sound. "I can't hear you all at once. I need you to talk one at a time, okay?"

The brownies fell silent. They all moved to the nest and trees and set down, so their wings' constant hum also died. The brownies murmured to each other, and then one flew back toward them and perched on Raven's shoulder.

"They need these sticks set up so they can build up around them," Raven said, pointing to some branches lying on the ground. "They want them off the floor so that the nymphs won't bother them, but they are having a tough time keeping them in place."

Penelope nodded. She pulled a length of rope off her belt and tied a loop to either end of the branch with most offshoots—they could use that to weave in more things. As she secured it in place, hanging from a tree branch, the brownies buzzed again.

"Not there. The rain always collects there," Raven said.

Penelope moved it to a different place, only to have the same angry reaction.

In the end, it took several hours to get the brownie sticks in the place where they wanted. Even then, they seemed to argue with each other over it all, but Penelope only shook her head and declared it the best she could do.

They gave Raven and Penelope berries, cautioning them to stay clear of the wettest parts of the forest due to kelpies hatching.

"That took a lot longer than I was expecting," Penelope said as they headed back out of the marsh.

"It was fun, though," Raven said, holding their hand out to Penelope.

She grinned as she took it and lifted it to her lips to kiss Raven's knuckles. Raven didn't particularly enjoy public displays of affection, but the two of them were learning what made the other feel warm and giddy inside. It surprised Penelope herself just how much she wanted to do things like hold hands. She'd never thought much about it before.

"We'll have to tell your parents to be careful in the swamp," Penelope said as they moved through the tree line into camp. "I know there are wards set up around to protect the students from kelpies but—"

"There you are!"

Penelope jumped as Jack and Marla came rushing over. Both of them looked stressed, and Marla wrung her hands together. They stopped just before the two teens, and Penelope suddenly felt like she was a little girl again, having snuck off during naptime.

"Where were you?" Jack demanded. "We've been searching for hours!"

Penelope winced. How had she forgotten the first rule of exploring a forest, especially an unknown forest? Always tell someone where you're going.

"We were just looking through the swamp for the Rattleback skin," Raven said.

"You should have told us," Marla said, dropping her arms.

"Sorry. We got caught up. There were some brownies and... Mom, Dad, I'm eighteen. Penelope's turning eighteen in a few months. We're fine. Why are you getting so angry?" Raven demanded, their voice tinged with defensiveness.

Penelope tugged on their hand slightly.

Marla made an angry noise in her throat. "We're not angry."

"It's my fault," Penelope interrupted. "I suggested Raven and I go look through the forest, and I forgot we had said nothing."

Both of Raven's parents turned to her with frowns.

"You're quite right that we should have said something so that you weren't worried," Penelope said, keeping her tone even. "I guess I just didn't think about how it would affect you, being used to traversing through the forest on my own. Next time we'll tell you."

Jack opened his mouth, then closed it.

"Next time, maybe we can come with you," Marla said.

Raven pulled away from Penelope. "I'm going to get supper started."

They headed off, and when Marla and Jack made to follow, Penelope cleared her throat. "Can I please speak with you?"

Raven's parents stopped.

Penelope gave them both a soft smile. "Look, I appreciate your concern. But Raven and I do need space, too. I know they don't want to say anything. They're always worried about how worried you are about them."

Marla nodded. "You have to understand; Raven has been poorly their entire life."

"But not anymore," Penelope whispered. "With everything that has changed, you all need to figure out where you stand with each other now. We will tell you when we go into the swamp. But we will go by ourselves sometimes. I hope you understand.

Neither of them spoke, although their expression said volumes. It must be tough for them to let go of the worry they'd had for their child for so many years.

Finally, Marla sighed. "You two need some privacy. We understand. Now let's go get some food, huh?"

She headed toward where Raven was setting out some food, shoulders slumped. Jack followed. Penelope took up the end, hoping that what she had said wouldn't hurt Raven's relationship with their parents.

CHAPTER

THREE

R aven glanced over their shoulder to where Mom and Dad were picking their way through the forest, with Penelope taking up the group's rear. It felt weird to lead their brief excursion, but at the same time, Raven enjoyed it.

The air was cool and heavy with moisture, with the scent of frost. Gnarled trees lined the path while thick undergrowth filled all the blank spaces. Moss grew on rocks and tree trunks. Everything was so green in here, even at this time of year.

Raven stole a glance over their shoulder to their parents. Mom and Dad moved carefully, picking their way over the ground. Since they were used to working in the hospitality business—running a hot springs resort—being out here in the wild paths of the Silent Marshes was an unusual experience for them.

The weight of Raven's argument with their parents the previous day still hung in the air, but at least they could all work together on this one. Maybe if their parents could see how easily they kept up with the demands of the swamp, it would be one less thing for them to worry about.

"Wait," Penelope called from the back of the group suddenly.

Raven came to a stop and turned around. "What's wrong?"

"This place..." Penelope looked uneasily around, a furrow in her brow. "Look at these plants. They seem too... wet..."

Even as she spoke, the surrounding ground seemed to ripple. Raven stared in horror and fascination as the plants and grasses swayed with tiny waves. As they watched, they realized that this wasn't solid ground. It only looked that way because the vegetation had grown so tightly over a pond's surface.

The black head of a horse peeked up out of the water, its ears flicking. It was as massive as the war horses Raven had seen when the military had training sessions near the hot springs. It's lips pulled back, revealing sharp, wolf-like fangs.

Kelpies usually didn't come out during the day... except in their birthing season.

It dodged forward, snapping its teeth and letting out a scream that made Raven's gill hair writhe. They leaped to stand before their parents, waving their hands over their head to stop the kelpie's charge.

A flash of light momentarily blinded Raven. Penelope's massive dragon form crouched around the group, wings circling them protectively. She roared, and a burst of fire ate up through the air toward the kelpie.

It disappeared beneath the water's surface, popped up several feet closer, and lunged for Penelope.

Images blossomed in Raven's mind, translating into disjoined words. Hunger in the belly. Young to feed. Danger. Go away!

Raven pressed a hand to Penelope's flank, silently telling her to stop as she sent an image back to the Kelpie, the image of their group turning around and leaving.

The kelpie drew to a sudden stop. It rose out of the water, a horse with seaweed hair, and stomped at the surface as its head swung back and forth. Its eyes latched onto Raven. A new image came to her mind: Penelope's flaming red hair and increased ache of hunger in the stomach.

Then images of little half-horse, half-fish creatures. The kelpies' babies. The image was Penelope in her dragon form, stomping and crushing at them.

Raven inhaled sharply, and changed the image to Penelope, carefully taking her natural form and walking away, making sure not to hurt any of the young. The kelpie snorted, pawing at the water again, but it seemed confused now.

"What's happening?" Mom asked, her tone stressed.

"The kelpie thinks that we're here to hurt her babies... no, only that Penelope is," Raven said, correcting themselves as they caught a new image.

Penelope, younger, dragging a bulbous mass of... something out of the water. A sense of panic accompanied the image, hunger clawing at their belly. Other images came hard and fast... Raven gasped.

Just as the brownies had been disrupted during the first year the witches came here, this kelpie was, too. Raven watched as its memories played before their eyes. Penelope had pulled its 'prey' from its nest, causing it and its young to go hungry. It hadn't been able to find more food, and other dragons had come and taken the young away...

Words wouldn't explain, but Raven tried to show the kelpie what happened after that. The Swamp Watch would have taken the young to another place where they could be fed, cared for until they were strong enough to be released again. Kelpies were an essential part of the ecosystem here.

Your babies would have been cared for, they tried to tell the kelpie, but it didn't seem to understand words.

"Pen," Raven whispered. "Take your natural form."

Penelope growled in her throat, but slowly shrank out of her dragon. She stayed protectively in front of the others, watching carefully. "Raven?"

"Trust me," Raven said. Their heart raced as they waded into the water and offered a hand to the kelpie, with the other hand on Penelope's shoulder.

They sent an image to the kelpie, hoping it would work. The kelpie's ears flicked backward, and it barred its teeth but slowly came forward, treading on top of the water.

"Mom, Dad," Raven whispered. "Put your hands on my shoulders."

"Raven—" Dad started but fell silent as they shuffled forward.

They placed their hands on Raven's shoulders as instructed, and Raven carefully enveloped them in mind-to-mind communication. The kelpie paused, snorted, and bravely closed the distance between them, nudging its head into Raven's palm.

As soon as they were all connected, floods of images flowed. It was an overwhelming conversation until Raven figured out how to put stops and valves in place, preventing all the thoughts and feelings from flooding through the connection.

The group stood there for some time, sharing images that ranged from Raven as a child to when they hovered in the inky black of the ocean staring into the vast, golden eye of the ancient Kraken Tidebreaker. Penelope shared other images of joining the kelpie in these swampy waters.

Raven frowned, but soon Penelope's intentions became clear. First, she would build a pen for the deer to protect them from predators. Next, she would let the kelpie feed on the deer's blood before returning them to the pen to recover.

Penelope ended the sequence with dragons watching the pen and providing the kelpie with fresh food.

The kelpie hesitated, then returned the image of it and Penelope gliding through the water together—it had accepted her proposal!

Raven nearly laughed aloud, giddy with relief. If they could keep working like this with the various creatures of the marshes, it would allow the Swamp Watch to better oversee the ecological situation.

Mom and Dad stood nearby, watching with expressions caught between trepidation and awe. Raven could see on their faces and feel through the bond that they were shocked, a little afraid... but also proud.

The kelpie moved away from Raven's hand and Raven let the connection between all of them fade out, careful not to cut it off too harshly.

Dad let out a shuddering breath as he dropped his hand to his side. "Is it always like that?" he asked, wonder in his voice.

"Not always," Raven admitted with a slight shrug. "But it's something that I've learned I can do. Why don't you two head back to camp? Penelope and I have a lot of work to do here, apparently."

Mom and Dad glanced at each other, and then they smiled. "No," Mom said. "We have work to do here, too. Now, where can that pen go? Over here, do you think?"

She gestured toward a spot of ground that looked pretty dry. Dad grabbed a stick and prodded the ground. Raven and Penelope glanced at each other as Raven's parents debated the pros and cons of the position.

"That went well," Penelope whispered to Raven, reaching for their hand.

Raven squeezed back, breathing out a sigh of relief. They had been afraid that their parents would react poorly to seeing just how much their child had changed... but now it appeared they were trying their best.

Raven winced. It had to be a tremendous change for their parents. Mom and Dad had dedicated so much of their lives to keeping Raven healthy, fighting to keep them strong even when their body gave out. They hadn't been fair to their parents and hadn't truly taken the time to consider how much of a change this must be.

"I'm going to stay with Marla and Jack to build the pen," Penelope said. "Why don't you and the kelpie go find some deer? It'll be a good idea to know where to start once we've got something put together."

"Yeah. I'll do that," Raven said.

They took a deep breath as they slipped into the water. Instantly, the hard coils around their gills released, and they drew off their hood for the feathery, almost hair-like gills to stream out around them.

The water was murky, but the kelpie circled and nudged Raven's hand.

Raven took hold of the kelpie's seaweed mane, and the two sped through the water, diving deep below the surface.

CHAPTER
FOUR

I t took several days to build the pen. But once Jack and Marla—
who had more experience in this matter than either Penelope or
Raven—decided that it was sturdy enough to hold a few small deer,
Raven relayed this information to the kelpie.

Penelope was eager for this experience to be resolved. While she
enjoyed spending time with the kelpie and exploring more of the intricate tunnels of water beneath the swamps, she was more getting restless to complete the quest and move to the next one.

Finally, they had a large, well-enclosed space where the little deer
could move around, graze, and otherwise enjoy themselves. The hunts
were successful, and soon they had a small herd for the kelpie to
choose from.

Penelope crouched near the water as the kelpie rested on the pond's
surface, with its little half-horse, half-fish babies scampering around it.
She couldn't communicate directly with the kelpie, but it had grown
more relaxed with her presence. She loved to watch it move; it was a
magnificent creature, that was certain.

"I hope this means you will not go after any more people," Penelope
said aloud as she straightened. "I would hate to be responsible for that,
even if you don't kill your prey."

The kelpie's ears flickered, and its babies disappeared under the water. The small herd of deer was currently grazing in a relaxed fashion as Raven wandered between them, touching one every so often.

They were undoubtedly explaining to the deer what the kelpie's intentions were. Penelope wasn't sure how it all worked, but the deer seemed to believe this was preferable. Penelope wasn't sure she'd enjoy being in the pen and fed on by the kelpies. Although if the alternative was to be hunted by coyotes and snakes, maybe she would.

"You ready to head back to camp?" Raven asked as they came to Penelope.

"Yeah. It's been quite a day."

The two of them headed toward the gate and carefully slipped out. It was up to the Swamp Watch to maintain this herd and the kelpies.

Penelope took Raven's hand as they headed back through the forest, swinging it lightly back and forth. Her shoulders were relaxed, which Penelope realized wasn't exactly normal these days. It seemed like she had so much stress; she was always tense.

But the feeling of accomplishment was too great for her to hold on to that stress.

"This went much better than I thought it would," Penelope said.

Raven nodded. "I'm glad that my abilities have been useful."

Something in their voice tipped Penelope off, and she glanced at her mate from the corner of her eye. "Are you all right?"

"Yeah. Mostly, at least." Raven sighed. "I'm glad we could help, but I really thought that I'd have collected the skin for my spell book by now. And even though I know these abilities are useful, not just for a state of emergency."

They trailed off and shook their head, their face veil wafting slightly as they sighed. Penelope kissed their knuckles, uncertain of how to go about reassuring them.

"Do you still regret going to springs at the Thunder Mountains?" she asked hesitantly.

"No," Raven said slowly, but there was hesitation in their voice.

Penelope moved a little closer. "What is it?"

Raven sighed. "I'm still getting used to this being my reality, I guess. I've made peace with this change, and I'm certain I have much good to do. But it's not what I expected to do with my life. And if I'm honest, it feels as though everything I wanted to do was taken from me, too."

"I..." What could she say to make Raven feel better?

"It's all right," Raven said quickly. "Most of what I wanted from life I knew I would not get, anyway, because of my physical condition. I didn't mean to be a downer."

Penelope frowned, not liking what she heard here. But even as she struggled to figure out what she should say and how she could reassure Raven, the water beside them rippled. The kelpie emerged, dripping water as it shook out its seaweed mane.

"Oh, hello," Raven said in surprise.

They dropped Penelope's hand to reach the kelpie, but it shook its head again and pranced away down a separate trail.

The two looked at each other, Penelope with raised eyebrows. Raven shrugged and followed the kelpie, which whinnied in a pony-like manner and trotted through two bushes. Penelope followed Raven, monitoring their surroundings.

When she stepped through the bushes, she gasped. They had come into a clearing, in the center of which lay a giant snake. Its skin was emerald green, with rows of rattles along its back. Its large, golden eye locked on the two of them.

The kelpie whinnied again, nudged Raven and disappeared back through the trees.

The Emerald Rattleback lifted its head and placed it back down, facing the two teenagers. It acted so docile that Penelope wasn't afraid as she slowly approached. Great patches of the snake's skin were loose on it; it was in the middle of molting.

"He wants us to help him shed," Raven said, striding to a patch of the skin. They started gently tugging on it, the flaky bit smoothly coming off.

Penelope was a little nervous about doing that, but it also worked. The Rattleback lay still as the two of them worked, and Penelope soon found herself in an easy rhythm. The skin came away smoothly, revealing fresh layers of even more vibrant scales beneath.

"He's saying that he knows that it's a witch's quest to gather the skin for their spell books," Raven said as they worked on the Rattleback's other side. "He likes to come out to the outer layers of the swamp and leave the shed skin for the young witches to collect."

"Oh," Penelope mumbled.

She knew the Rattlebacks were intelligent, but she hadn't known they were this intelligent. It made her wonder about that first year here in the Silent Marshes and the students' interactions with the Rattlebacks. How aware had they been of the situation?

Before she could ask, though, Raven made a noise in their throat, sounding worried.

"What is it?" Penelope asked, pausing in her work.

Raven looked up. "Hmm?"

"You just sounded worried."

"Oh." Raven shook their head. "Oh, it's just that the Rattleback is saying he's concerned about the weather. It's much earlier in the year than he usually sheds. It's been overly warm and dry this winter, and he's concerned about the health of the swamp."

Penelope nodded. Everyone all across Eldavon was concerned about the dryness they were experiencing. Several of the neighboring kingdoms also had very mild winters. While it meant that the harvest and growing season had been lengthened, the biggest concern was the possibility of a drought coming.

But Penelope was sure that the weather would right itself soon. And if not, there was always magic to take care of the fields and rivers, right?

"Pen, how long does the skin last before it's not useful anymore?" Raven asked.

"I don't think it has a time that it stops being useful," Penelope replied. "I mean, the skins are collected in our first year, but the books aren't put together until our fifth year."

"That's good. He was concerned that by shedding too early, the skin would be useless," Raven replied.

Penelope nodded once. She considered asking the Rattleback if he knew about what happened during their first year here, but decided against it.

Soon they were done and had armfuls of skins. Most of this they left in the clearing but kept a bunch that they planned to scatter around in other sections of the marshes. And, of course, Raven would keep the amount they needed for their own spell book.

They returned to camp in time to see that Jack and Marla had made supper. Penelope's stomach rumbled, and she quickly cleaned up.

Once the four of them were at the table, they passed around the food and ate.

"The cabins are all clean, and the students are due to arrive tomorrow," Jack said as he plopped mashed potatoes on his plate. "And I see you got what you came here for."

Raven nodded, and Penelope tried to imagine their beaming smile. "The kelpie led us to an Emerald Rattleback as we were heading back. I guess since we helped her, she helped us. It really makes me wonder just how interconnected everything is. It's like the Rattleback and kelpie could have their own communication."

"Is that something you'll want to look into more?" Marla asked.

Penelope chewed on a piece of carrot, considering Raven. What if they wanted to do something like that? So far, the two of them hadn't talked much about what they planned to do after graduation, other than Penelope's determination to join the military.

Raven needed to have their own goals, though. What sort of wants did they have that they thought they had to give up because of their condition as a gorgon?

"Maybe," Raven said.

Their parents smiled at their child, and Penelope suddenly felt like she was intruding on a private moment.

"Whatever you decide, know we're proud of you," Jack told Raven. "This experience has shown us how much you've grown. And no, it's not easy for us to acknowledge that... but we are very proud of the adult you've become, Raven."

Marla reached across the table and took her child's hand. "So very proud. You're remarkable, and we know that you'll make it far in life."

Raven made a noise that sounded both embarrassed and pleased. "Thanks. And I know it's hard for you to realize I have changed. But thank you for trying."

Jack and Marla beamed at Raven. Penelope smiled into her food. Good. That was another quest that they'd succeeded in—the quest to be acknowledged as 'no longer a child.'

CHAPTER

FIVE

R aven led Penelope into the one long cabin just outside the Golden Forest. Penelope used her free hand to feel the space around herself, though she gripped Raven tightly. Raven grinned widely, their face hurting with their smile.

"Can I take this blindfold off now?" Penelope asked.

"Almost," Raven promised as they got her into position.

They glanced to where Mike and Ellen, Penelope's parents, had arranged the presents around a cake. Ellen was just finishing up lighting the candles. As Raven brought Penelope to stand before the table, their smile grew wider.

"All right," they said, "you can take it off."'

Penelope took off the blindfold, and her parents burst into a rendition of 'Happy Birthday.' Raven hummed along, not really liking to sing —they had little voice. Penelope blinked as she looked over the presents and cake, her cheeks flushing.

When the song was done, and Penelope had blown out her candles, Raven hugged her. "Looks like we're going to be eighteen together for a little while, at least."

It was bizarre how just a few months' difference would have put them in entirely different years for their trips to the Silver Springs.

Penelope laughed and took a seat at the table. "I thought we would take today to get settled in."

They had only just sat down when a handful of glittering creatures came in. They fluttered about, tiny creatures with long, lizard-like bodies, curling tails, and colorful wings. Chameleon Sprites.

Raven grinned. They were looking forward to meeting the sprites. Everything they had heard of the little creatures had made them seem extraordinary.

The sprites hovered together and flew around Penelope and her parents, making happy chittering noises. But when one of them drew near Raven, it suddenly let out a frightened squeak, and they all bolted. They hid beneath the various tables set up in the space.

Raven winced.

"It's okay," Penelope called, though her glance was to Raven rather than the sprites. "Don't be afraid."

The sprites crawled from under the tables and gathered in one long, vertical line. They glowed, and the illusion of a tall person with curling hair and blue eyes appeared.

"What is it?" the sprites asked, pointing at Raven.

Raven winced and sucked in a deep breath. "I... I'm a gorgon. I drank from a spring in the Thunder Mountains, and I became this."

The sprites tilted their head this way and that as they studied Raven. "You are not like the others. You taste salty."

Sprites sensed emotion, not facial expressions, so Raven knew the veil couldn't hide their true feelings. Their heart beat faster and the familiar bitterness rose in their throat.

They were used to other people's uncertainty, but these little creatures were said to be among the most innocent in Eldavon. Was this just fear of the unknown, or did they sense the danger that posed?

Raven inhaled deeply as Penelope tried to explain what a gorgon was to the chameleons. She spoke so rapidly that she was tripping over her own words—did she sense the feelings that hovered under Raven's surface?

"You are distressed." The sprites focused on Raven. "Why?"

Raven cleared their throat. "I'm upset that I frightened you."

The sprites gingerly stepped forward, bobbing the head of their illusion this way and that as though trying to get a better look at her. "Hmmm. You are, aren't you? So why did you do it?"

"Well, I didn't mean to," Raven said dryly. "I can't help what I 'taste' like. Gorgons like me are water-based creatures, so maybe I taste like salt to you. But you need to know that when I look at creatures without this veil, they turn to stone—so you absolutely cannot sneak up on me or try to take it off, okay?"

Sprites were mischievous little creatures, and she wouldn't put it past them to try something like that.

The sprite-illusion nodded thoughtfully. "We will tell the others."

The illusion broke apart, and the sprites scattered like they were running for their lives. Raven's gut twisted as they turned back to the table, trying their hardest not to let the others know how deeply this interaction had upset them. It wasn't as though the sprites were trying to be upsetting.

"Well, I'm glad that I could tell them before they tried to prank me," Raven said, forcing their voice to be bright. "Let's have cake!"

Penelope continued to give Raven a worried look, but shook her head and tried to school her expression once Raven pushed a present toward her.

As she was opening the present, Ellen cleared her throat. "So after this, you plan on heading to the Thunder Mountains, correct?"

"Not until summer," Raven corrected. "Pen and I are going to spend a few weeks at the Institute for me to sit in on the second-year witch's classes after I've got the paper from the Phoenix Ginkgo."

Ellen nodded.

"And then next year is going to be your final year at the Institute," Mike said as he served out pieces of cake.

Raven took theirs and held their veil a little from their face to eat it.

Penelope lifted out a thick book from her present. "Is this the collective poetry of Willa Sapphere?" she gasped. She squealed as she jumped up and leaned across the table to hug Mike, then Ellen. "This is exactly what I wanted!"

Penelope's parents beamed at her.

"This one next," Raven said, picking out the present they had gotten Penelope.

"So, Raven," Ellen said as Penelope carefully picked apart the wrapping; she was so meticulous that they had to have a conversation while she worked at it. "Have you decided what you'll be doing after graduation?"

Raven winced, though they tried to hide it. "Um... for the time being, no. I'll go with Penelope wherever the military posts and figure out what to do once we know where we'll be."

"You'll be going right into military service, then?" Ellen asked, sounding shocked.

Penelope's hands froze.

Raven swallowed hard—hadn't Penelope told her parents about this already? From the reaction between the three of them, they had accidentally opened up a can of worms. They eyed both Penelope and her parents warily.

"We were planning on it, yes," they said, trying to keep the nerves from their voice. "Even though we have resolved most of our issues with Odentia, the other kingdoms also have unrest. We figured it would be better if we could get right at helping to resolve the problem."

Mike and Ellen glanced at each other, the worry evident on their faces.

"You've both been having such an intense few years, though," Mike said, folding his hands over the table. He hadn't touched his cake. "It might be better for you to take some time off and maybe travel around or explore your options before settling down into such a demanding career."

Penelope put the present aside. "What's that supposed to mean?"

"Raven's options," Mike clarified, holding up his hands. "I didn't mean you should look at other careers, Pen. We both know that you've decided on a military career. We just—"

"All right," Penelope interrupted. She shook her head hard. "Let's just not talk about this, okay?"

Mike and Ellen agreed. They started picking at their food again, but it was all half-hearted. Penelope didn't even start opening her presents again.

Raven folded their hands in their lap, wishing they knew how to go about this. This was an old wound. To begin with, Penelope had told them how her family had reacted to her decision to join the military.

"All right," they finally said, straightening. "The mood had completely been killed here. I don't think that sitting in silence is helpful at all."

Penelope glanced at them through the corner of her eye, shooting a warning look.

"You might not want to talk about it. But it's important to finish this conversation at least, especially since nobody is enjoying the cake or presents anymore," Raven told her.

Penelope scowled and ducked her head.

Raven sighed as they leaned forward. "We have already discussed possibly taking a gap year or even a few months before Penelope signs up with the military. We've decided against it. We'll look for housing together as soon as we know what camp Penelope will be assigned to."

"You're both so young," Ellen said, her voice soft. "Mike and I both took two years just flitting about at odd jobs before we settled on the Fire Watch."

"But I'm not you," Penelope said.

"Honey, we're not saying that this is what you have to do," Mike said, sounding frustrated.

Raven cleared their throat. Just like how Penelope intervened in their fight with their parents, they felt like they owed her to play mediator here. "I believe I have a better understanding of what's going on here."

Both parents and Penelope turned to them with hopeful expressions.

"I know that you have had pressure and stress in your relationship before because Penelope decided to join the military," Raven said slowly, formulating their thoughts as they spoke. "I think that's probably why you're having the knee-jerk reaction now, right?"

Penelope grimaced but nodded. "Probably."

"And you both are worried about Pen," Raven said. "Regardless of your acceptance."

Ellen sighed as Mike nodded.

"But this isn't just about the military, is it? There's something else," Raven prodded, staring hard at Penelope's parents.

They might hear Ellen and Mike's thoughts if they pushed even a little harder. But peeking into someone's head without their permission seemed insufferably rude. Raven turned away, breaking the budding connection. No, they needed to share their words, not be spoken for.

"There is more," Ellen agreed. "I didn't mean to imply that you two were making a poor decision or that you needed to change your mind."

"That's what it sounded like."

"I didn't mean it like that," Ellen repeated. "I just wish you'd had time to figure yourself out without these high stakes that have been put on you. I feel you didn't have the chance at a proper childhood."

Penelope sighed as she rested her chin on her hand. "I don't feel like I had a proper childhood, either. But there isn't anything that we can do about that."

Sorrow radiated off Penelope's parents as they picked at their cake again.

No, there really wasn't anything they could do to fix it. Raven wished they knew what to do... but remained silent now, not knowing how to improve the situation.

CHAPTER
SIX

P enelope stretched her arms over her head, enjoying the cool spring morning. Yes, it felt more like a summer morning, but she would not let herself worry about it right now.

Raven, Penelope, and her parents had spent a lovely day wandering in the forest. The Chameleon Sprites played a few light jokes on them, seeming to have gotten over their initial reaction to Raven. They hovered about as the group walked idly through the trees.

The few leaves left on the trees whispered in a light breeze as sunlight filtered through the branches overhead. The ground was littered with coverings, leaves that were still as bright as if it was autumn. Scrub brush lined the paths with old, dried berries still on them. Birdsong drifted through the air, although Penelope wasn't sure if the birds were real or if it was the sprites.

Soon enough, they came to the sacred Phoenix Ginkgo. Momma sighed happily as she laid her hand on the side of the tree. It was bare of all leaves at this time of year, and its bark glowed a pale orange-gold under the sunlight. Even without its leafy crown, it looked magnificent.

"It's been too long since I've visited this place," Momma said, closing her eyes.

Da stepped up behind her, wrapping his arms around her waist as he nuzzled her neck. "Maybe we should take the next year off, then. Take a leave of absence and do some traveling."

Penelope ducked around the massive tree to the other side, where Raven stood with both hands pressed against the tree trunk.

"Quick, if we hurry, we can get away while they're too busy necking to notice," she said in a stage whisper, just loud enough for her parents to hear.

The two of them laughed and made loud, fake kissing noises. Just enough to make Penelope feel a little nauseated. She was glad that her parents were still madly in love, but she didn't want to think about them with all that kissy stuff.

Kissy stuff. Am I ten?

Raven turned their face toward her. They wore a red face veil today, and with their brightly colored orange and yellow robes, they looked like a part of the forest.

"I don't know how to harvest the wood," Raven said, ignoring Penelope's joke.

Penelope's face fell.

"I worked with Professor Avery to do this, but I can't. I don't have the right magic," Raven said, dropping their hand to their side. "I can't get the wood I need for my pages without hurting the tree."

Momma and Da rounded the tree.

"I can help you." Momma suggested. "I still remember how. You were able to do it with Professor Avery, weren't you?"

Raven nodded.

"Then maybe you need to connect with me—" Momma cut off.

A dozen Chameleon Sprites slipped through the trees to linger just beyond them. Penelope waved as they formed the illusion of a stout woman with flowing black hair. They lifted their illusioned hand in greeting, and Penelope waved back.

"What are you doing here?" she asked politely.

"We have been talking," the illusion replied. "And we would like to help you. We have an idea to create a new world for you. All of you, so you can see what it would be like if Raven was not a gorgon. Maybe it will help you know how to harvest the wood," they added.

Penelope tensed. They didn't need to know what a world with Raven as a non-gorgon would be. They were a gorgon, and there was nothing wrong with that. "That won't be necessary."

The illusion drifted closer, forgetting to walk. "We heard last night, too, how your birthday wish was to have another childhood."

"That wasn't my wish," Penelope protested, but even as she did so, another thought came to her.

Despite everything, she struggled with these feelings of being paired 'just because.' If she could see what a world with Raven as a human was like, and be able to relieve some of those childhood days, would she be able to be a better mate?

"What exactly are you suggesting?" Raven asked, sounding interested in the whole thing.

The illusion woman smiled and bobbed her head. "We can take you into a dream and weave it together so you are both in the same world. There, we can nudge what you know and help you see what could have been."

"But it would still all just be in our minds?" Raven asked doubtfully.

"Yes."

"So it wouldn't actually show us what it would have been like," Raven said.

The illusion sighed heavily. "Except we have asked the forest, and it's told us what would have been. Do you wish for this dream or not?"

Raven turned their veiled face toward Penelope. Penelope looked to the sky. The last time they were here, the sprites had given her a vision of everything she'd wanted. But it had been shaky, unbelievable.

Would going into the dream willingly be at all useful?

She turned to her mother. "Will you come with us?"

Raven seemed to sigh—in annoyance? In regret? Were they happy Penelope had made this choice, or were they angry?

Momma's eyes widened. "You want me to come into your dream as well?"

Penelope smiled at her, nodding. "You're the one that said you wished I could have had a better childhood. I'd love for you to come with us."

Momma smiled back. "I'd love to."

Penelope took a deep breath and turned back to the illusion woman, straightening herself. "I accept, then. My mother and I will go into this dream world. Raven?" She glanced at her mate. "Do you want to come?"

"I... guess so," Raven said doubtfully. "But before we start this, I need to make sure that you won't see what I look like now. I don't care if it's in a dream or not, and I won't want to take any chances."

"Of course," Penelope said fervently.

The sprites jumped from foot to foot, like they couldn't hold in their excitement. "All right! Let's get this going. Oh... what about that one?" they pointed at Da.

Da laughed as he raised his hands into the air. "I'll decline the invitation. I know you don't always understand time the way we do. So I'd like to keep an eye on everything from this side to make sure that they're not trapped in the illusion for too long."

The sprites shrugged, then instructed the three to sit around the ginkgo tree. Penelope settled down into a comfortable position between two roots. Nerves jangled through her, but she was excited, too. Even though she couldn't believe it was entirely accurate, she hoped to get some answers.

"Close your eyes," the sprites said as they moved apart, breaking the illusion of the woman. "Breathe deep and let your minds empty."

Penelope's eyes drifted shut as a pleasant warmth flowed through her. Glitter drifted down over her face and a sweet smell filled the air.

When she opened her eyes, she was fourteen years old, standing in the middle of her second-year camp at the Golden Forest. Classmates dances about with laughter and chattering to each other, but it all seemed just a little vague.

The knowledge that she was an adult, and this wasn't real lingered in the back of her mind. But when she took another deep breath and let it out, she could also let herself forget that.

Professors Avery and Delphine stood before the students, standing tall and proud with the backdrop of beautiful greens and golds.

"We're only here for a few weeks," Professor Avery boomed, his voice carrying easily. "I expect you all on your very best behavior."

"Where are the sprites?" Kaia whispered next to Penelope. "I want to meet them!"

Penelope gave her friend a half-hearted smile. While she knew she shouldn't be, she couldn't stop thinking about the matching ceremony that would be held at the end of the year. It seemed so strange to her that they would all learn who their fated mates were.

But there was an uneven amount of witches to dragons. How would they all have a mate if there was an extra witch?

"Pen, are you okay?" Wickham asked on her other side. His face pulled in concern.

Penelope shook off her thoughts. She had never thought much about who her fated mate would be one day, and the last thing she wanted to do was to obsess about it now. The stars would know who her perfect match was; she just had to trust them.

"I'm fine," she said with a grin. "I was just wanting to go play tag."

The beating of wings suddenly sounded overhead. Penelope looked up to see her mother's magnificent dragon form glide in from the sky with Raven on her back.

Momma's not a dragon. She's a witch.

Her father's magnificent dragon form glided through the sky, with Raven and her mother on his back. He swept down, and allowed Momma and Raven to slide off, then launched himself back into the sky.

"Sorry we're late," Momma called as she strode forward. "We had to briefly discuss some details they got wrong with the sprites."

Professor Avery nodded wisely. "It's good to have you here."

Penelope's eyes landed on the slim figure that walked just behind Momma. Her heart raced as her breath caught in her throat.

Even though this was just an illusion, she knew it didn't accurately represent what was real. The whole instance of Momma being a dragon, then suddenly it being Da, was proof of that. But she couldn't help but eagerly lean forward.

Raven said that they didn't want to be seen as how they currently were. But was Penelope finally going to see what they once looked like?

CHAPTER

SEVEN

R aven kept their jacket pulled over their head, heart shallow in their chest as they headed into one cabin. They weren't sure if excitement or trepidation filled them as they shut the door. Penelope had tried to follow, but Ellen had pulled her back. Raven found it odd that the two of them were separate like this but was grateful for the time they'd had to talk.

A full-length mirror hung at the back of the cabin. Shivers ran down Raven's spine as they approached it.

They crossed the room to stand in front of it, then slowly dropped their jacket.

Their hair was short, soft, and mousy, the way it had been before they drank from the springs at Thunder Ridge. They were younger, too, with more baby fat on their cheeks and a chin that wasn't as pointed as it was these days. They gazed at the mirror, taking in their nondescript brown eyes, their thin lips, and small ears.

To their surprise, they found that the face looking back at them was exactly the same as the one in their memory. And it didn't seem that different from the one they had now. Their shoulders relaxed as a knock came on the door.

"Raven?" Penelope called. "Can I come in?"

Raven reached for their jacket, heart jumping to their throat again. But even as they did so, they froze. Ellen had already looked into this face and hadn't turned to stone. The sprites had reassured them that even if they were to show what they looked like now, it wouldn't have any effect, as this was only a dream world.

Another twist came to their stomach. Did they really want Penelope to know what they looked like? They were unremarkable. Was it worth it?

Raven shook their head. Penelope had already accepted that she would never see their face. They could share this now, and when they visited Mom and Dad at the hot springs, Penelope would see the family pictures. Those had Raven's face painted in them.

They crossed the cabin and opened the door, slowly at first but finally with a sudden gust at the end, as though they were presenting themself to the world.

Penelope jumped slightly at their dramatics but laughed as they entered the cabin, eyes cast down.

She looked so young. Raven had a hard time thinking that even just a couple of years would make such a difference... but it certainly did.

"So, here we are, a couple of fourteen-year-olds in our second year," Penelope said.

The reality of being a gorgon was always present in Raven's mind, an intricate tapestry of identity and myth, but the whole illusion of normalcy remained. Being a gorgon was just one part of their existence, they thought. But here and now, they could set that aside to play this game.

Penelope shuffled on the spot and looked at Raven's feet. "Can I look at you?"

"I don't know. I'm not sure that I like the idea of you seeing me as a fifteen-year-old whenever you imagine my face," Raven joked, but their nerves were clear in their voice.

"Yeah, I'm pretty sure I won't do that," Penelope said, smiling but keeping her eyes downcast. "But if you don't want me to look, I won't."

Raven's heart melted toward Penelope. More than once, their dragon mate had told them she wished she could see their face. Looks weren't important to Penelope, but she found it disjointing not being able to read Raven's facial expressions.

Raven took a deep breath, bracing themself. "You can look."

Penelope lifted her eyes. She studied Raven's face, her eyes first taking in all of them, then studying each feature. She reached out and touched Raven's cheek. "Is this what you look like now?"

"No. This is what I looked like then."

"What changed?"

Raven turned aside and led Penelope to a bench where they sat. Raven rubbed their arms, cold despite the warmth of the day outside of the cabin. "It's hard to explain. There was my hair, of course, and that was the most dramatic change."

Penelope nodded.

"There was more, though. My cheekbones and chin grew more prominent, but my face got fuller, anyway. I was always extremely thin, but I put on muscle. So much that I didn't know what to do with it at first," they laughed.

"And this was a problem?" Penelope asked, frowning.

Raven considered how to answer. "It didn't feel like my body. I was used to feeling a certain way of knowing my limits. Suddenly, it was like I didn't know myself anymore. It was frightening, if I'm honest."

"I guess I can understand that. It took some getting used to how my body feels when it's in dragon form."

"My eyes changed, too. They're still brown but grew more... intense, I guess." Raven let out a shuddering breath. For a long time, they refused to look at themself in a mirror, afraid that the old stories where gorgons would turn themselves into stone if they saw their own reflection was true.

Eventually, though, it was too much. They had to look. Herja reassured them she had found no information showing that they'd turn into stone. In the end, they hadn't.

"One day, maybe I'll draw you a picture of what I look like now, or give you a more detailed description," Raven said, shaking their head. "But not today. Today, I want to throw myself into this illusion as though it's our last hope. I want to pretend like I really am a witch in my second year, and we don't know that we're mates."

Penelope pinched a strand of their hair in her fingers. "Witches have silver hair."

Raven glanced at the mirror, and now they had silver hair. They had to stifle a giggle. The sprites really took this seriously, didn't they?

A knock came on the door, and Icarus poked his head into the cabin. "We're going to have lessons on how to get the wood for the spell books."

Raven and Penelope glanced at each other, then hurried outside. They joined hands as they walked over to where the rest of the class was sitting. Raven ignored the rule that dragons weren't meant to participate in the training, as Professor Avery stood near the Phoenix Ginkgo.

"This is how we get the wood out of it," he said, looking over the group awkwardly in a manner that didn't fit the professor Raven knew. "We use our word magic. So I go like this," he turned to the tree and cleared his throat. "Hey, tree, give me a chunk of wood."

Penelope snorted. She looked around, presumably for her mother, but didn't see her anywhere.

Raven paid close attention to what Professor Avery was doing. Even though they had stood in classes on word magic, that wasn't something they had done themselves; their magic seemed more based on forging connections. It wasn't something that they could use consciously.

A gash opened in the tree's side, and a chunk of wood dropped out as though the tree had spat it out.

"Good, thank you, tree," Professor Avery said. "The thing about this word magic is that you must connect with everything around you. That's the point of this year, learning how everything is interconnected. Tree, please heal."

The ugly gash closed up.

Professor Avery beamed at them all. "Now it's your turn. Find a tree and talk to it."

Raven frowned as she glanced at Penelope. The others wandered off at once and immediately got their trees to spit out chunks of wood.

"Connections," Penelope said as she headed toward a large, ugly apple tree. "The Golden Forest is supposed to be highly interconnected. But we saw that the Silent Marshes were connected, too. There's got to be something you can use in that, right?"

"I'm a witch," Raven said uncertainly, not knowing if now was a good time to play the game or if it'd be better for them to approach this as a gorgon. "The only way I'll find out is to try, right?"

Penelope nodded with an encouraging smile.

Raven sat down, looking up at the apple tree. They reached out and pressed both hands to the trunk, trying to feel the energy there. Trees didn't have minds, not like animals did. So how were they supposed to connect to this?

Penelope stretched out on the grass as Raven talked to the tree, trying to convince it to give up its wood. Nothing worked.

Eventually, Penelope stood and took Raven's hand. "Let's take a break. No, let's play hooky. We can explore the forest and get in trouble for staying out too late."

Raven frowned.

"Please?" Penelope asked with a wink.

She looked so excited about the possibility of playing a game like this. Raven didn't have the heart to say no. They nodded, and Penelope pulled them into the forest, leaving their classmates behind.

It was a wonderful day. They never got tired or hungry, and there was always something interesting to see. They played hide-and-seek. They went swimming. They climbed trees and serenaded birds. When the sun sank and bathed the land in a golden twilight, the two headed back to camp.

Ellen was waiting, cooking a large pot of food. She smiled widely at them. "Did you have a good day?"

Penelope ran to her mother and threw her arms around her. "It was wonderful!"

Raven smiled as they sat down at a table. It really was.

CHAPTER

EIGHT

Penelope wasn't sure how many days they spent in the illusion. All she knew was that as soon as one day ended, the next started. While they occasionally worked on their lessons with Momma rather than the fake Professor Avery, Raven and Penelope spent most of their time in the forest being carefree kids.

As wonderful and freeing as it was, however, as more time passed, Penelope itched more and more to get to the regular world. There was so much they still had to do out there.

Childhood didn't last forever, and it was time to grow up.

She rolled over and opened her eyes, then cried out in surprise. She was no longer in the Golden Forest at all—she was in her dorm at the Institute. It took her mind a moment to catch up, to realize this was still the sprites' illusion.

Kaia bounded in, dressed in a beautiful, frilly ballgown. "Hurry, Pen! It's the day of the bonding ceremony. We're going to be late!"

Penelope opened her mouth to protest. Why would they have to go through this again? But she closed it again. Maybe it was something that Momma had requested from the sprites.

Shaking her head, Penelope swung out of bed and found the same plain dress she had picked for the bonding ceremony two years ago. It was pretty but simple and lacked the frills and ruffles that Kaia's fashion had.

Not that the frills and ruffles suited Penelope. She liked her simple style but wondered if she wasn't feminine enough.

Shaking her head, she put on the dress and headed out, expecting to see Raven. To her surprise, the dorm was empty. Even Kaia had mysteriously disappeared, leaving Penelope wandering the halls alone.

"I don't know what the point of this is," she said aloud. "I already have been through the ceremony."

She rounded a corner that led toward the library and found herself in the dining hall. The tables were all pushed to the sides, and a large stage was set up in the middle of the room. All of her classmates were already there, beckoning her to join them.

Penelope found herself oddly nervous as she ambled to the stage. She searched their faces, but didn't see Raven. Her heart beat a little faster.

"What's going on?"

"Our bonding ceremony," Herja said with a dreamy-eyed look that didn't suit her.

Penelope's stomach clenched. Suddenly, she couldn't do this. She turned on her heel and ran where she had come, escaping the fake ceremony room. It wasn't real—so why was she so nervous about it?

But where was Raven?

Tears burned in her eyes as she hurried on, her head bowed. She was so rushed that she didn't realize she had made her way outside until she suddenly ran into someone wearing overalls.

"Oof!" Penelope grunted as she fell back. She looked up to see Momma staring down at her.

"Pen? What are you dressed like that for?"

Fresh tears spilled down Penelope's cheeks. Didn't the sprites know that her family would be here for it if this were real? "The sprites are playing at a fake bonding ceremony. I ran away."

"So that's what they were after," Momma murmured. She shook her head as she sat on a bench that had appeared. "Come sit with me, Pen."

Penelope slumped beside her mother and snuggled into her side, the way she hadn't for many years. She wiped her eyes, trying to get herself back under control.

"I wish it could be real," Penelope whispered. "So I could know for certain."

Momma stroked her hair back from her forehead, resting her cheek against Penelope's head. "Know what, baby?"

Penelope inhaled sharply, looking around to make sure Raven wasn't secretly behind a rosebush. Her gut twisted. She hated to say it out loud, even if it was the fear lingering ever since she and Raven had danced under the starlight on Thunder Mountain.

"I wish I knew Raven was really my perfect match. That I wasn't just thrown in with them because they needed someone, and I was there," Penelope said in a rush, but it wasn't enough. She had to say more. "Everything has changed, Momma. Ever since I went to the Silver Springs."

Momma froze, eyes wide and startled.

"I was going to be a dragon, and I knew that. And I was, but nothing else has happened the way I wanted it to," Penelope said, bunching her hands into fists. "Every year, there's something that causes trouble. Every year, I find myself in a life-and-death situation. And I know it will only be more intense once I join the military."

Momma let out a shuddering breath.

Penelope shook her head, trying to get her thoughts in order. "I wanted nothing more than to be part of the Fire Watch. Then it became apparent I couldn't... because I was needed elsewhere, and the good of the kingdom came first."

"Pen—"

"No, please don't interrupt," Penelope begged.

Momma swallowed and nodded.

"Then, when I went through my second year, I didn't worry about who my fated match was because I knew I'd have one. But I didn't. Then I met Raven, and we got our star threads in the most random way."

She trailed off, the burst of energy draining. "I love being a dragon, Momma. I always wanted to be one, and it feels right. But it also feels like I got one wish, only for everything else to be messed up."

"I know it's difficult, but you can't think that the stars made a mistake in putting you and Raven together."

"I don't think it was a mistake—I think it was an afterthought," Penelope admitted. It was the first time she had said the words aloud, and even though it made shame bite into her stomach, she couldn't take the words back.

"Oh, my darling." Momma hugged her tightly.

"I hate feeling this way. It feels like a betrayal to Raven," Penelope whispered, tears spilling down her cheeks.

"You two seem to be so happy together, though."

"We are. And I love them. I really do. I just can't shake this feeling." Penelope pulled away, wiping her face again. "Maybe it's because I spent a year without a mate, thinking something was broken within me. I don't know."

Momma pulled out a handkerchief and mopped up Penelope's tears. "And why do you not want to go through this ceremony with them now?"

"What if..." Penelope hesitated, unable to say the words. It was only an illusion that the sprites created to make them all happy. But what if she and Raven weren't bound together when they went through the ceremony?

Momma seemed to understand all the same. "Is there anything I can do?"

Penelope shook her head miserably.

Momma sighed as she hugged Penelope tightly. "I think you should do it, Pen. I understand the fear, but I think it would be good."

Penelope shook her head again. She didn't want to go in there. She didn't want to face everything that she feared. But what sort of dragon didn't face their fears? Reluctantly, she took a few deep breaths to calm herself and stood.

But even as she stepped back toward the Institute, everything rippled and disappeared.

Penelope's eyes opened.

She was no longer nestled in the roots of the Phoenix Ginkgo, where she had been when she fell asleep. She pushed herself to her elbow, blinking in confusion as she looked around. Was this part of the illusion? It didn't feel like it, but how had things changed so drastically?

Da kneeled beside her, handing her a waterskin. "Here, drink. It's been a couple of hours."

Only a couple? Penelope didn't feel thirsty until she drank and then gulped down the water as she realized she was parched.

Momma was stirring a little ways away from her, but where was—

Ah. Raven was tucked in against Penelope's side, their face veil laying lightly over their face to reveal the shape of their nose. They made a slight noise as they woke up. And as they did so, Penelope realized something else...

The blanket Raven had woven, with their star threads glittering silver throughout it, lay over them. Penelope touched the blanket, running her fingers along one of the fine threads. A chill was in the air, but under the blanket, she and Raven were toasty warm.

Penelope's heart swelled with an overwhelming sense of gratitude as Raven stretched out beside her. Despite her challenges and uncertainties, she couldn't deny their connection.

All at once, she knew that every one of her doubts was unwarranted. She'd filled her head with too many thoughts instead of simply accepting what had happened.

Her mate hadn't been there when she went through the bonding ceremony. She had had to find them, and at the first opportunity the stars got, they had rectified that.

Tears of joy welled in Penelope's eyes as she pulled Raven into her arms, embracing them tightly.

"I'm glad you're in my life, Raven," she whispered to her mate. "I love you."

Raven made a surprised noise but relaxed into Penelope's embrace. "I love you, too."

As they hugged each other, laughter filled the air. Dozens of sprites zipped here and there over their heads, sending showers of glitter down on them. As Penelope watched them move, a thumping noise suddenly appeared beside them.

Her eyes widened as she glanced over. Beside Raven, a slender piece of wood seemed to have been extracted from the Phoenix Ginkgo. She could feel the magic flowing through the surrounding forest, yet another remembrance of how interconnected this place was. The thin gash where the wood had extracted itself from the ginkgo closed in on itself, leaving smooth bark behind.

"Oh," Momma said in surprise as her eyes widened. "I've never seen it do that before."

"It does it all the time," the sprites said above them. "How else do you think we have so many to plant? It gives a little piece of itself, and we take that piece and put it somewhere else, where we need to have a fire tree."

Raven picked up the chunk of wood tenderly in their hands. "Thank you."

"We thought you needed it, so we gave it to you," the sprites replied.

Penelope grinned. "Yes, we did—thank you. For everything."

CHAPTER
NINE

Spring came to a sudden, screeching end while Raven and Penelope spent the last semester at the Institute. Usually, there would be a few weeks of gradual warming, some rain, then the beautiful greens of spring followed by bright flowers.

Not this year. It appeared Raven simply woke up one morning to find themself in the dead of summer.

"It's so muggy here," Raven sighed as they stood in the little ravine at the base of Thunder Ridge.

While the Institute had held a dry heat, these stormy mountains had so much moisture clinging to the air that Raven almost felt as if they threw back their hood; their gills would be free to unfurl and catch the liquid in the air. That might be preferable—breathing in this humid heat was difficult.

Penelope grunted in her reply, lying in the shade of a canvas they had set up as a lean-to. The tent was simply too hot to live in, even though they'd have to take shelter inside if it rained. Pen hadn't been sleeping well since the heat wave started.

"Sorry you're not feeling well," Raven said, wincing as they glanced at their mate.

Penelope's usually tanned skin was red as her hair. She lifted a hand and waved it vaguely, then sighed. "I suppose we should start up the mountain."

Raven sat next to her. "I thought we could wait until nightfall. It'll be nicer to travel at night and hopefully that will mean the rocs won't see us coming."

They were on their ultimate quest before the start of their final year. If they had known they would be placed with the witches, Raven would have grabbed a roc feather when the others had gotten theirs. Unfortunately, that had all been so new then that none of them had thought about it.

Now they sighed as they hugged their knees to their chest.

They had arrived only yesterday and set up a neat little camp for the days they would be here. It had been storming steadily since then and only broke half an hour ago.

If it weren't for the heat and the threat of the rocs, Raven would have agreed that it was wise to start now. Though She and Raven were made for water, they supposed a storm wouldn't make that much of a difference.

They sighed, and Penelope propped herself up on her elbow. "Do you need to talk about it?"

Raven turned to her in surprise. "Hmm?"

"Something is bothering you."

Raven winced. They turned their face back to the mountain, gazing up at it. They couldn't deny that part of their reason for staying here was the fear of setting foot on that mountain again. It felt like they knew every tree and crevice, but it was still terrifying.

"I'm just afraid, I guess," Raven admitted quietly. "This is where it all started. It's like facing my mistakes without knowing if they were actually mistakes or if I was guided here by something else."

Penelope rolled to her stomach, resting her head on her arms. "What do you mean?"

"We never would have met if I hadn't come here. I wouldn't be a gorgon, we wouldn't be fated mates... or maybe we would, but we never would have met," Raven repeated with a shrug. "Maybe the stars brought Finnegan to me so he could bring me here. I don't know."

"Maybe," Penelope said. "I like to think that it was the sea, however. It needed its seer back and so chose you."

That was a nice thought; Raven had to admit. They wondered how accurate it was... but then, that was an answer they would never get.

"At least I know how to use my powers better," they said, trying to pull their thoughts to a more positive place. "With any luck, I'll be able to connect with the rocs and make this an easy quest. All I need is one of their discarded feathers."

Penelope nodded, but a strange look came to her face as though something had occurred to her.

Raven stared, forgetting Penelope couldn't see their face. "What?"

"Well, I just remember how the rocs saw your face and didn't turn into stone. Like Tidebreaker, and the kelpie."

Raven shivered. "That's what I'm most afraid of—that we'll come across those poor creatures I turned to stone."

"Didn't the Crown take them back to the palace to figure out how to undo it?" Penelope asked, sitting up now.

She frowned. The red was seeping from her face, which was a good thing, Raven thought. Then, the air was growing rapidly cooler—a storm was coming. They bit back a sigh and focused on Penelope's words.

"They did, but so far nothing's worked. From what I understand, the water from the Silver Springs seems to do something, but they're not sure what." Raven buried their face into their knees. Despite not knowing what would happen, they still felt ashamed about the first months in the mountains.

It started to rain, and Raven stood. Yes, this was what they wanted.

"Can you make sure that I've got dry clothes to change into when I get back?" Raven asked, turning to Penelope. "I can't breathe—I'm going to stand in the rain for a while."

"Sure," Penelope said.

Raven strode into the thickening rain, removing first their face veil and then their hood. As the rain thickened, the coils of scales around their gills released and opened up, feathering through the air. They grabbed the water droplets as they fell, and Raven felt like they could breathe.

Being in water felt so good and right. They closed their eyes and turned their face to the sky.

They weren't sure how long they had stood there, embracing the sky, before they sensed Penelope's agitation. She was getting worried about them.

With a reluctant sigh, Raven turned back to the tent, covering their face as they did so. They let their gills remain free as they returned to the tent and ducked inside. Penelope's relief was palpable, but she only handed them their dry clothes and told them a towel was in the curtained-off area.

Raven retreated behind the curtain to dry off and dress in fresh clothes. Once they were done, Penelope helped them hang their wet things across the middle of the tent, and each lay down on their own narrow bedroll.

"I feel like going in the storm is going to be the best time," Penelope said, resting her head on her arms once more. "We'll be able to contact the rocs easier when they're active—or rather, you will. But I don't want to get wet."

"I'm fine waiting here until nighttime," Raven said gratefully.

Penelope rolled over and stared hard at Raven. A light stone glowed overhead, allowing them both to see clearly in the tent.

Raven didn't like the look on Penelope's face. It seemed like she was thinking of something perhaps a little too deep... although Raven wasn't sure why they had that feeling. Only they were confident they wanted Penelope to stop thinking about whatever they were thinking about.

They searched for something to discuss with Penelope but thought of nothing.

So they stayed silent.

"Raven?"

"Yes?"

"I want to kiss you. May I?"

Raven shuddered. "No. You might see my face. I will not let you do that. It's not worth the risk."

"What if we turned off the light?" Penelope asked, her voice sad, as though she already knew the answer.

Raven turned their back to Penelope. "What if there's a flash of lightning? Even if you closed your eyes, you could open them again. You wouldn't even have to do it on purpose."

"But you could lift your veil to your nose Or blindfold me. I wouldn't mind that."

"No."

Penelope was quiet momentarily, then asked, "Is it because you don't want to risk me seeing your face, or is it something else?"

Raven resisted the urge to turn back around and snap. "What else would it be?"

"I don't know. Simple lack of attraction. Not wanting to have any sort of physical relationship." Penelope's voice was soft, sad, but resigned. "If it is, that's all right. And if it's not just because you're worried about me seeing your face, that's all right, too."

Raven was quiet. If it was all right, why was she bringing it up?

"If it is because you're afraid, then maybe we can work around it," Penelope continued. "If it's something else, though. But it's okay if you need to have this conversation end now. As long as we talk about it again sometime."

"I don't want to talk about it right now." Raven let out a heavy sigh as they closed their eyes. Kissing. The truth was, they wanted Penelope to kiss them, too. They wanted it so much that it made their eyes flood with tears.

But it was too dangerous. And both of them were going to have to live with that.

CHAPTER

TEN

The night was so filled with thunder and lightning that neither of the teens would risk getting fried by a random lightning strike. Instead, they stayed in the tent and switched between card games and Penelope reading aloud until they were both exhausted and fell asleep.

The next morning, the clouds remained tight around the mountain's peak, making the day cool and wet—just the right weather for a gorgon and water dragon to hike.

They talked animatedly about the story they were reading. It was one that Herja had written, and reluctantly handed over to allow them to read, so long as they gave actionable feedback when they were done.

Raven enjoyed the story. It was a little more simplistic than Raven expected, and sometimes the phrasing got too flowery for their taste, but it was enjoyable all the same.

The conversation faltered when they came to a cleft in the rock. Two enormous cliffs stood on either side of a slight dip, where fallen rocks piled into a towering structure.

"Is this...?" Penelope trailed off.

Raven let out a shuddering breath. "It's the spring. Where Kaia brought the overhang down and buried it."

Penelope reached for Raven's hand. "Should we leave?"

Raven hesitated. While they hated to be here, the memories plagued their mind; the mountain had deliberately stopped them from getting here again after that first drink. Had it brought them back? But for what purpose?

"I think... I think I need to face this. I need to make peace with what happened to me. The transformation. How different my life is. Maybe to tell the mountain that I'm grateful for the gift?" Raven shook their head doubtfully.

What were they here for?

"I thought you made peace," Penelope said, her voice low as she squeezed Raven's hand.

"I thought I did too. But maybe all I did was accept it without facing it?" Raven let out an aggravated sigh. That made little sense, but they weren't sure how to get their thoughts across in words.

Instead, they approached the massive pile of rubble, letting memories of when they drank wash over them.

"Finnegan carried me up the mountain. He was kind. Or at least, I thought he was. He talked about how he knew what I was going through as a sickly child. He told me about how his brother saved him, how he just wanted to make him proud."

Penelope wrapped her arm around Raven's waist.

"When we came here, he left me to drink because he'd left our food lower down. I drank... the change happened. And I ran away, feeling something in my gut that I was no longer safe."

"In your gut," Penelope repeated. "Or was it the voices in the springs?"

Raven tilted their head toward her in confusion.

"Kaia said she heard voices in the springs, asking for respite. Do you think maybe those voices warned you?" Penelope frowned as she reached out to touch the stones. "Do you think you could reach through and find them? Maybe we could get more information about the spring."

"Like what?"

"Like, this place is far, far from the ocean, and yet it turned you into an ocean being," Penelope said, lifting her eyes. "It's worth a shot, isn't it?"

She had a good point. Raven rubbed their palms against their trousers as they considered it. They'd worn long pants because of the coolness of the day but had shorts in their backpack. Wouldn't it make more sense that they would have been turned into a gorgon by an ocean spring?

Raven hesitated a moment longer, then nodded. Perhaps they were thinking too much about themselves in this. Maybe the mountain hadn't brought them here because they needed to face anything about themselves—perhaps they just needed more answers.

"Do you mind if I bring you with me?" Raven asked, turning to Penelope.

Penelope flashed them a grin. "I'd be offended if you didn't."

Raven gazed at their mate, gratitude welling in their heart. Then they reached through their connection, linking Penelope to them in mind-to-mind. They closed their eyes as they reached through the rubble with their mind, searching for any sort of consciousness that they could connect to.

A dimness seemed to surround them, and Raven's eyes snapped open. They gasped, their jaw dropping open when surrounded by a circle of veiled, hooded figures. Their heart jumped to their throat, and they clung tighter to Penelope's hand.

"Are you seeing this?" Penelope breathed.

The beings seemed to shiver, then shake themselves. One of them stepped forward, veiled face turning toward Penelope.

"The dragon has no place here," the figure said. "She is not one of us."

"She's my mate," Raven replied, holding Penelope's hand tighter. "She's a part of me. Therefore she's a part of this."

Another of the figures laughed. Raven got the sense that this one was a woman. She shook her head as she lifted her hands to the others. "Young Raven has a point there. Come now; we've been waiting for centuries. Let's not drive away the newest of our number."

Penelope shuffled on the spot and shot Raven a nervous smile. Raven swallowed as they looked around them.

"What is this place?" she asked. "I mean—who are you?"

"We are the gorgons of long ago, we who stand between the doors of life and death," the first figure that had spoken intoned. He—and he was a he, Raven got that sense from him—bowed his head toward the ground. "We who served our long years have found our rest."

The woman laughed again. "What my verbose colleague means, we're dead gorgons. One unique gift that follows us through to the afterlife is that we can connect back to living gorgons."

"But you spoke to Kaia. She's a witch," Penelope protested.

The woman lifted her hand and wagged a finger in the air. "We connected to Kaia through Raven here, Pen. We weren't about to let Finnegan get these powers. The poor lad wouldn't be able to handle it."

"Did you reach out to me to drink?" Raven asked, looking around at the circle. There were so many of them... "Did you pick me?"

"In a manner of speaking," the woman replied. "But not in the way you're thinking. I know; it makes little sense. But you'll figure it out, eventually. That's not why we brought you here again, however. Magic holds a delicate balance in this world, and something is disrupting it."

There were nods at this statement. A chill washed over them. "What is?"

"We don't know, just that there has been an ebb for some time, which is why we chose now to create a new gorgon. We're sorry that it was on you, Raven. It's a heavy burden."

Penelope looked at Raven, worry clear in her eyes. "Can you tell us more about what's going on, so we can be better suited to face it?"

The woman sighed. "I'm sorry, we really can't. There's only so much that we know as dead people. All we know is that there is an imbalance. But steps have already been taken to help balance it back... both of your efforts with Lyra and Tidebreaker, for instance."

Steps taken.

Raven pulled Penelope closer to their side, feeling strangely defensive, as though they needed to protect her. If that whole situation with

Tidebreaker and Lyra was just one step to bring balance back into the world, what did that mean for what would come next?

"We know you're frightened," the man said, stepping forward as he lifted his hands. "And I wish this burden wasn't put on one so young. Just remember, you were made for this world—this world wasn't made for you."

"We ancient ones made big mistakes," another of the ancient gorgons said. "We puffed ourselves up and thought we were invulnerable. It led to our downfall."

"I certainly don't think this world was made for me," Raven said emphatically. "All I want is to help others."

"And you have that chance," the woman said.

Penelope looked around at all of them. "What about me? What role am I supposed to fill in all of this? I'm supposed to be Raven's mate and defender. But if they're bringing balance back to the world."

"Not by themself," the woman replied. "Goodness! That would be far too much pressure. So your role is what it always was, Penelope. To be their mate and defender."

Raven felt them slipping away. "Wait! I have so much more to ask you!"

"We've kept the doors open as long as possible," the woman said. "The rest is up to you."

Raven called out once more; then, the figures faded away. They looked around, frustration welling through them. What sort of answer was that? What had been the purpose? To show up and tell them cryptic things and then—

Penelope hugged them tightly.

The action shocked Raven out of their spiraling thoughts. They swallowed, then hugged their mate back. As they did so, they considered the words the gorgons had said.

They had been chosen for a reason. There was an imbalance of magic in the world. And even if nothing else, that was something they didn't know before.

"What do you think they meant?" Raven asked as they pulled back.

Penelope shook her head. "I don't know. But we'll figure it out, Raven. Together."

As Raven stared at their mate, a sudden longing washed over them. Was it really so dangerous to think that they couldn't even kiss? Penelope had given options. Did Raven really believe that they were so dangerous as to never—

Before they could finish that thought, thunder boomed overhead—and the rocs screamed.

CHAPTER
ELEVEN

The rocs circled overhead, their massive wings creating gusts of wind as lightning flickered between their feathers. Penelope was rooted to the spot, unable to stare at the magnificent sight above them. They were divine creatures; she wanted to throw herself to the ground and beg for their succor.

"Penelope," Raven shouted beside her.

Penelope could just tear her eyes away from the magnificent creatures circling overhead. Raven clutched both sides of her face as rain pelted down on them.

A roc swooped toward them, talons outstretched. Penelope grabbed Raven and swung them both to one side, narrowly avoiding being caught. They tumbled down the steep slope, limbs and clothes tangling until they abruptly stopped.

The air was driven from Penelope's lungs.

"Cover your face," Raven shouted as they scrambled back. They yanked their hood off and turned their face to the sky.

The rocs screamed again. Penelope closed her eyes as Raven pulled off their face veil.

The screaming stopped. The beating of wings continued to circle above them, and Penelope kept her eyes tightly shut. Her heart slammed into her ribs as she listened, desperate to know what was happening.

Something light brushed across her face. Her eyes snapped open as a feather as long as her arm came to rest beside her.

Raven was just tying their face veil back into place. When they turned back to Penelope, they chuckled and held out a hand.

"Were you able to connect to them?" Penelope asked, eying the sky warily. It was clearing up like it hadn't been violently stormy two seconds ago.

"Sort of. They want us to leave and not come back. Apparently, we're too old to be welcome around here. They only tolerate the children because they don't fight back," Raven said. They bent and picked up the feather. "They seemed to know what we wanted, though."

"Er... good?" Penelope said, still wary.

Raven shook their head. "After the conversation, we had just had with the gorgons? I'll take it as a win. At least we don't have to keep climbing."

Penelope nodded as they started back down. "And," she added, "we have yet more information to help with the Institute's third-year students when they come here. The rocs don't consider them so much of a threat."

"But they would rather be left alone. It might be something that I can work with here, too," Raven said, picking along the path carefully. "Negotiating between the Rocs and the Institute."

Penelope nodded her agreement. So much had happened over so little time that her mind was reeling, but it also made sense. The gorgons said magic was becoming imbalanced. Raven could work as a negotiator to create communication between beings where there was none before.

How better to restore balance than to allow Eldavon to see where they were taking advantage of the natural world? Just like they had been unknowingly party to a great injustice forced upon the krakens, the same sort of thing could be happening all across the kingdom.

Penelope nodded to herself—it made sense. Raven wasn't supposed to bring the balance back all by themselves. They were meant to provide the tools the kingdom needed to restore the balance.

"The rocs didn't turn into stone," Penelope said. Going down the mountain was much quicker than going up. "Neither did the kelpie or Tidebreaker. I wonder why that is. Maybe creatures with enough innate magic are immune."

"Maybe," Raven said, sounding deep in thought.

Maybe dragons were, too. But Penelope would not bring that up. Not now, when there was so much more to discuss. Besides, she knew that testing out the theory wasn't a risk Raven would take. Penelope wasn't willing to risk it, either. Not until the Crown figured out if they could reverse the magic.

"I wonder if they might know what it does and how it works," Raven said, turning back toward the mountain's peak. "Maybe if I could understand more about how it works, I could stop it from happening."

The longing in their voice was obvious. Penelope winced—as sorry as she felt for herself, unable to see her mate's face. She had forgotten about what the effect on Raven was. How much worse would it be to suddenly have your face be a danger to others?

"I guess it's one of those things that we'll have to figure out as we go along," Penelope said.

The two resumed their journey back down the mountain, both lost in their own thoughts.

There was so much that they still didn't know. A shred of doubt filled Penelope's heart. Was it right for her to decide to leap directly into military service after graduation, after all? Perhaps it would be better for her to take a gap year, as Momma and Da suggested.

The two of them could spend time figuring out more about Raven's powers. They could stay at the Institute—Penelope could get a job as a janitor or something—and have the wisdom of the professors and Headmasters helping them figure it out.

Or they could go back to Tidebreaker. It was an ancient kraken. Maybe now that Raven knew more about what questions to ask, Tidebreaker could give more answers.

It was a possibility, at least.

"What are you thinking?" Raven asked suddenly.

Penelope looked up in surprise. She hadn't realized that she had slowed her pace considerably. "I'm just wondering if maybe I should put off joining the military so that I can help you find more answers once we graduate."

Raven hummed. "I've been thinking about that, too. But I'm not sure. The kingdom still needs you, Pen. And with the unrest happening, we will need to protect ourselves."

"Yes... but is it better to open up communication?" Penelope asked, stopping entirely again. "You're a communicator. I'm supposed to support you in that role. If I'm in the military, then I'll be stepping toward fighting as a solution. Intimidation, at least."

Raven took her hand and brought it to their clothed lips. "Or, as part of the military, you will be better positioned to help me get into negotiations, where I can help to facilitate communication."

"That's... true."

Penelope sighed. The military of Eldavon wasn't just about fighting and defense. They often ended up helping in various natural disaster zones, cleaned up after floods, evacuated people in the face of fires, and carried supplies to offer to other kingdoms.

Maybe it was just because she had been put into a position where she was in danger and fighting for her life so often that was where her mind went. And if it was, maybe she needed that gap year for therapy. Going into a potentially explosive situation while feeling like a lighted match wasn't a great idea.

"You know what's great, though?" Raven said, their voice light as they tugged on Penelope's hand, pulling them back toward camp.

"What?"

"You don't have to make that decision right now."

Penelope opened her mouth, then closed it again. For some reason, she had forgotten that, she had always been so sure of her choices until now.

A weight lifted off her. That was right. She didn't have to make the choice right now. She could focus her energy on Raven to help them through all these recent revelations they had faced.

Because that was what a mate was supposed to do, and they belonged together, the two of them. They were perfectly matched.

Penelope grinned and walked a little faster again. "You're right. Thanks."

"Welcome."

"So, we got this thing much faster than we expected." Penelope nodded toward the feather. "Where do you want to go next? We've got a few weeks before your parents are expecting us."

Raven hummed. "I think... I want to stay here for a few days. Just you and me, with no quests or pressure to do anything or be anyone."

Penelope grinned. "That sounds wonderful."

"It's decided, then. We'll stay for a few more days." They lifted their face to the sky. "And I think the rocs will just have to tolerate our presence."

CHAPTER
TWELVE

That night, they sat for a long time under the stars, talking about their journey or in silence. A fire crackled merrily, providing a warm glow to their small, damp campsite. The sun hadn't come out all day, and while the coolness was a relief, it turned a little too cool as night fell.

The flames turned to coals, slowly blinking out one by one. They would have to smother the remnants as soon as they retreated to the tent, but Penelope found herself reluctant.

It had been a magical day. Her mind buzzed with everything that had happened, and she knew sleeping would be difficult. The weight of it all pressed upon her, leaving her restless despite the peace she'd felt earlier in the day.

"Penelope, I have something that I need to tell you."

Penelope turned to Raven. They were little more than an outline in the darkness, but their voice held trepidation. Something about it made Penelope's stomach clench.

"What is it?" she asked, trying to steady her voice. She didn't want Raven to feel like they couldn't talk to her.

Raven moved closer, their presence a soothing comfort. They sat down beside her and took her hand, their fingers intertwining. "Today changed everything. I mean, we've grown; we've discovered so much about ourselves and the world. But we have a lot of questions left unanswered. And I'm not sure we'll ever find those answers."

"I know what you mean. We shouldn't tire ourselves out. Momma always said that if we're exhausted, sleep before our brains turn to mush."

Raven snorted. "A fish on a water wheel?"

"Visualize it."

After a moment, Raven hummed. "You know? That works. But regardless of what has happened today, there is something I haven't told you."

"All right," Penelope said nervously.

Raven stroked their thumb over Penelope's knuckles. "This transformation I went through. I know now that it was for more than just me; I have a job to do here in Eldavon and the world beyond it. But I'm not sure I will ever be okay with what happened."

"You mean becoming a gorgon?"

"Yeah. That change happened to me. I don't think I'll ever be fully comfortable in my own skin."

Penelope's heart sank at Raven's words. She understood the weight they carried, the burden of their transformed body, and the uncertainties that came with it. She tried to think about what it would feel like if she had become a dragon, without knowing that she had always wanted this...

No, that was the wrong way to look at it. If she had become a witch instead of a dragon. Would she have felt comfortable looking in the mirror and seeing silver hair instead of silver eyes?

She squeezed Raven's hand gently. "I think it's normal to feel that way after everything we've been through. We've seen and experienced things that most people can't even fathom. It's changed us, inside and out."

Raven sighed, their breath mingling with the night air. "I know. But whenever I glimpse my reflection, it feels foreign. Like I'm wearing a mask, even when it's just me."

"I..." Penelope trailed off, trying hard to think of what she could say to make her mate feel better.

"This isn't a problem you can fix," Raven told her, interpreting her silence correctly. "I just thought I should let you know. Because if I'm supposed to be the communicator, I should communicate."

Penelope smiled slightly at that joke, then sighed. "If we're talking about things we need to communicate, I have something myself."

"All right," Raven said, sounding worried.

"I want to see your face," Penelope blurted. "I want to see what you look like. I want to kiss you without you feeling afraid. And I know it's not possible right now. I will not push it. But once the Crown has figured out how to reverse your stone magic—"

"What if they never do?"

Penelope caught herself, took a deep breath, and shook her head. "Sorry, I didn't mean to say it like that. If they figure it out, I want to try something. I think dragons might be immune to your magic, like the krakens and the rocs."

"Pen..."

"It's just a theory. One that I will not test unless we know for sure that it can be reversed," Penelope whispered. "And it's not something I wanted you to carry around. I love you, Raven. I will be satisfied to be with you in any way I can be. Whether I ever see your face."

Raven let out a shuddering breath. "I guess I already knew that. You've accepted it, but that doesn't mean if there comes a time when you might see me...."

"I love you," Penelope repeated.

"I love you, too." Raven laughed, a soft, reflective sound. "You know, being a gorgon isn't something I would have chosen for myself. But it's a part of who I am now, regardless of whether I am comfortable in my own skin or not."

"I wish I could help with that."

"I know."

Penelope lifted their hand to her lips, kissing their fingertips. "And I know that any further discussion about revealing your face, whether or not I can see it, will have to wait until later. But even if we can never kiss... I'm glad you became a gorgon."

65

Raven let out a surprised-sounding noise.

"If you were never a gorgon, you never would have come into my life," Penelope said, leaning forward. She rested her forehead on Raven's. Despite the cloth between them, she could feel the soft swirls of her mate's breath. "I would not ask for more."

"I love you," Raven said again, but it felt like it held something deeper this time.

A promise, maybe. One day, when they knew themselves better, maybe things would change. Perhaps they wouldn't. But regardless of what the future looked like, they would be together. They were meant to be, bound by the stars.

And Penelope knew they'd be able to face every challenge and decision. Because they'd be together, and that was all that really mattered.

"I love you, too," Penelope breathed, and in those words, she put a promise of her own.

"I will always be by your side. Every mountain to climb, every valley to wander. Until we are old and gray.

"Every ocean to cross, every day sitting and darning socks," Raven replied, "until we are old and gray."

They sat like that, their foreheads pressed together, as the last of the coals died away. Above them, the stars shimmered and danced merrily in a sky free of clouds.

THE END

If you enjoyed this book, please consider leaving a review on
Goodreads, Bookbub or your favorite retailer.
Reviews help me reach new readers.

Read *The Quest for the Cursed Mirrors*, the fifth and final book in the *Defenders of the Realm* series!

Join my newsletter for writing updates, sneak peaks, review copies, sales, and giveaways!
www.mhlebeault.com

www.ingramcontent.com/pod-product-compliance
Lightning Source LLC
Chambersburg PA
CBHW050903120626
46554CB00003B/995